Llamas in pajamas

Russell Punter

Illustrated by David Semple

Sam, Ali and Charlie
all yell with delight.

Please come to my
sleepover.

Frankie

There's a creepy sleepover
at Frankie's tonight.

They pick out pajamas
with stripes...

spots...

and dots.

With their packs on their backs,
off to Frankie's they trot.

Into Frankie's big bedroom
run three jolly llamas.

"Hi guys!" shouts Frankie.
"Check out my pajamas!"

Charlie's
look silly.

And Frankie's
are blue.

They play games by flashlight.

"Woo-hoo!" Frankie wails.

"Let's stay up till midnight,
and tell spooky tales."

They whisper of spirits that shiver and shake,

and quivering monsters,

until it's so late...

...they fall fast asleep,

but wake with a jump.

"The floorboards are quaking!"

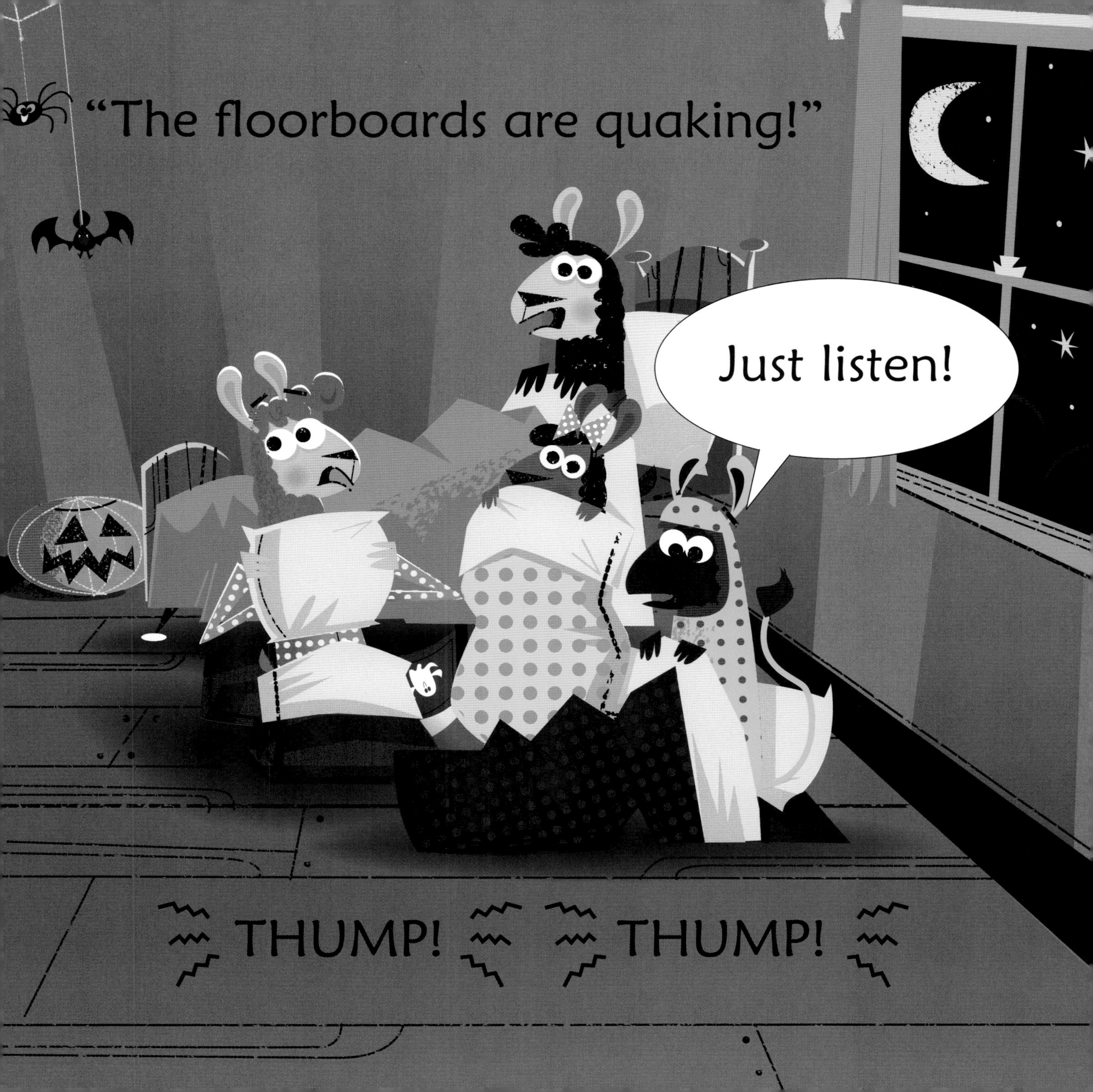

"A beastie is coming!"
"He's haunting the hall!"

"Take cover!" calls Frankie.
"Or he'll eat us all."

BUMP! BUMP!
CLUNK! CLANK!

He's outside the door!

They hide under blankets
and slide to the floor.

CREAK! goes the door.
It opens a crack.

In creeps...

...Frankie's grandma
with a great midnight snack.

About phonics

Phonics is a method of teaching reading used extensively in today's schools. At its heart is an emphasis on identifying the *sounds* of letters, or combinations of letters, that are then put together to make words. These sounds are known as phonemes.

Starting to read
Learning to read is an important milestone for any child. The process can begin well before children start to learn letters and put them together to read words. The sooner children can discover books and enjoy stories and language, the better they will be prepared for reading themselves, first with the help of an adult and then independently.

You can find out more about phonics on the Usborne Very First Reading website, **www.veryfirstreading.com**. Click on the **Parents** tab at the top of the page, then scroll down and click on **About phonics**.

Phonemic awareness

An important early stage in pre-reading and early reading is developing phonemic awareness: that is, listening out for the sounds within words. Rhymes, rhyming stories and alliteration are excellent ways of encouraging phonemic awareness.

In this story, your child will soon identify the *ll* sound, as in **call** and **jolly**. Look out, too, for rhymes such as **spots – dots** and **jump – thump**.

Hearing your child read

If your child is reading a story to you, don't rush to correct mistakes, but be ready to prompt or guide if he or she is struggling. Above all, do give plenty of praise and encouragement.

Edited by Jenny Tyler and Lesley Sims
Designed by Sam Whibley

First published in 2014 by Usborne Publishing Ltd., Usborne House, 83-85 Saffron Hill, London EC1N 8RT, England.
www.usborne.com Copyright © 2014 Usborne Publishing Ltd.